COMPLETE BY MYSELF

Stories of Women's Resilience, Renewal and Rediscovery

DR. USHA DUBEY

Clever Fox®
PUBLISHING
Chennai • Bangalore

CLEVER FOX PUBLISHING
Chennai, India

Published by CLEVER FOX PUBLISHING 2026

ISBN: 978-93-7500-515-5

Dedication

To my grandchildren - Ipsit, Swanik, Nirvan, and Neil,
whose innocence, wonder, and pure joy remind me of all that is
beautiful in this world.

PREFACE

What happens when a woman stops waiting to be completed by someone else and chooses to complete herself instead?

'Complete By Myself' is a beautiful collection of stories by Dr. Usha Dubey, that explores the silent struggles, hidden strength, and fearless reinvention of women who dared to redefine their lives. From unspoken sacrifices to unfulfilled dreams, from heartbreak to healing, these stories reveal how women discover resilience in the face of loss, courage in moments of silence, and freedom in choosing their own path.

Whether stepping into midlife with newfound boldness, embracing second chances, or blooming late after years of restraint, each story carries the same truth: A woman's wholeness does not depend on anyone else.

Poetic, raw, and deeply relatable, 'Complete By Myself' is more than a book — it's an awakening for every woman who has ever felt incomplete.

CONTENTS

HER SKY, HIS EARTH

I was frustrated because, in spite of my good marks in science, I was allotted the humanities stream. In our school, streams were assigned in class 9 based on the marks obtained in the previous final exams. It was true that my marks in languages were also quite strong, but my dream was to become a scientist. In my immature mind, arts subjects seemed meant for weaker students, not for toppers who ranked within the first five in class.

I was sitting with a sullen face when Sumit, my neighbour and classmate, decided to add fuel to the fire. "Why do you girls want to take up science when you will end up in the kitchen, anyway, spending your time with pots and kettles?"

It was like salt on an open wound. I glared at him and snapped, "Do you think cooking is derogatory? If so, stop eating from today."

He looked impassive and replied, "Of course not. Cooking requires a lot of intelligence; that's exactly why you should not waste it on studying science."

"You are incorrigible," I shot back.

Our families lived on the same campus, and we were classmates too, though always at loggerheads. To me, he was a pompous, self-opinionated boy who believed females could never be equal to males. According to him, women needed protection and were meant to remain at home, taking care of the hearth. Yet, apart from this so-called male ego, he was otherwise affable, helpful, and caring. Sometimes his mother would joke that perhaps we had been siblings in a past life and had not gotten along, so God made us neighbours in this one—but that did little good, for we still fought like siblings.

The very next day, Father went to school and requested the principal to change my stream. Though the principal believed I was better suited for languages and would excel in humanities, my request was granted, and I was moved to science.

School life, despite these tussles, was fun. Every teacher had a nickname known only within our group. Bunking classes was not the norm back then, but we occasionally committed that sin when lessons grew unbearably boring.

After school, all of us went our different ways. Some joined the same college, while others chose different institutes. I pursued my M.Sc. and was soon in search of either a job or a PhD opportunity at a reputed institute. Luck favoured me when I was selected for research work with a scholarship at a well-known university. My dream of working as a scientist had finally begun to take shape.

Sumit had gone into engineering. Though we knew of each other's whereabouts, life carried us along different currents and we drifted apart.

In the meantime, my parents had begun searching for a suitable match for me. They asked if I had any specific conditions.

"Only one," I said firmly. "I will not give up my work as a scientist under any circumstance. For the rest, I trust you to find me a good family."

In due course, I got married. After the wedding, I moved into my in-laws' home and continued with my job. My husband worked in a corporate position that required frequent travel. Life settled into a routine. About a year later, I took a short leave to spend time with my parents. They were delighted to have me home.

My mother, with a smile, said, "It is so good you came now. Sumit is getting married next week. His mother wants you to attend your childhood friend's wedding."

The next day I went to meet aunty. She was overjoyed to see me. I had always been close to her, and she often said she never missed having a daughter as long as I was around. Soon, she asked me to lend a helping hand with the wedding preparations, since there was so much work to do.

"Of course, aunty," I said warmly. "But where is the groom? I need to congratulate him."

She laughed. "He will arrive just a day before the marriage so he can save his leave for after the wedding."

"Aunty, who is the bride? One of his classmates?" I asked curiously.

"No, the girl was selected by us," she replied, "but Sumit has given his consent."

"That is surprising, aunty," I said with raised brows. "As far as I remember, he always had a very fixed image of women and their behaviour."

Auntie smiled and said, "We asked him first if he had someone in mind, but he denied and told us to go ahead."

"So, he has become a gentleman, it seems," I said laughing. Aunty smiled.

After two days Sumit was there, and I congratulated him. He pretended to be surprised and asked why I was congratulating him instead of sympathising with a sacrificial goat.

"You know I am going to lose my independent status," he said.

"That means you are going to adopt your wife's surname," I teased, "because it is the woman who gives up her original name and is usually known as Mrs. so and so for her whole life. If you are going to reverse it, then I applaud you."

He made a face and I said, "I haven't changed much. Even after being a scientist, I do spend time with pots and kettles too."

He said he was not in a hurry to marry as he didn't find any woman of his choice, but as his mother wanted him to settle down and he felt his choice in a life partner was perhaps impractical, he let them make a choice, which was quite good, and agreed to tie the knot.

I reminded him of a hilarious classroom incident, and we laughed a lot. It was Hindi period, and sir was explaining a famous couplet that contained some Urdu words: *"kisi ko mukammal jahan nahi milta, kabhi Jami to kabhi aasman nahi milta".* Sumit as usual, was inattentive and looking outside. Suddenly the teacher came near him and asked loudly, "You tell me, what is meaning of kabhi jamin to kabhi aasman nahi milta?"

Not to be outwitted, Sumit said he could give one example to explain it. "And what is it?" The teacher growled.

"Well sir, birds." Now we all were curious and, suppressed our smiles.

"Well sir," Sumit said, "birds fly in search of food but can't stay for long in sky. They come to land for food but can't stay here either, so they make nests. So, they can't get either *zameen* or *aasman* always."

The whole class burst in to laughter, and even sir couldn't help his smile. Remembering it, Sumit said he remembered how I explained the meaning of those lines later, and, turning serious, said he now understood the depth of these lines better. The marriage took place simply, without much pomp and show, and I instantly liked his wife, Dharitri. She was good looking, graceful and the best thing was the love for books, which we both shared. We shared some common interests such as literature and favourite colours. But at the back of my mind, I had a nagging feeling that her hobbies and priorities were not the same as her new husband's.

The time for my return had come, so I bid goodbye to everyone and in private told Sumit he had found a wonderful life partner, and I hoped he would take good care of her.

"Of course," he said, giving me a quizzical look. I understood his surprise and replied lightly, "I meant, don't expect her always to be busy with pots and kettles just to satisfy your gluttony."

Time passed swiftly. Between my job and family responsibilities, especially after the birth of my two children, I hardly had a moment to spare. My mother told me that after retirement, Sumit's parents had moved back to their native place, and in due course they lost touch with everyone.

Nearly eight years later, I had to travel to a nearby town for official work. I stayed in a guest house, and in my spare time decided to visit the central library. The staff kindly arranged it for me. Libraries always filled me with awe. The knowledge and imagination of centuries preserved within their walls were enough to make me feel both small and inspired.

After settling into a comfortable corner, I looked around and noticed a lady and a gentleman engaged in deep discussion. Something about the woman's face felt familiar, though I could not place where I had seen her before. Suddenly, she rose to leave. Our eyes met, and a flash of recognition in her gaze confirmed my hunch. She walked quickly toward me and exclaimed, "Ambuja! So nice to see you after so many years! How are you?"

It was Dharitri, Sumit's wife. But then, who was the man standing behind her? Following my questioning glance, she turned, paused, and then said calmly, "Meet my husband, Rajiv."

I was stunned and stared at the man. He looked affable, though not striking in appearance. His large eyes were full of warmth and compassion. Sensing my awkwardness, he excused himself politely, saying he had some urgent work and would join us later.

The moment he left, I turned to Dharitri. She met my gaze steadily and said with composure, "I walked out of my previous marriage within two years. It did not work out."

"Tell me everything," I urged.

For a moment she was quiet, lost in her thoughts, and then she began.

"Things were alright in the beginning. At times, he would tease me about my cooking, telling me to learn from his mother how to make his favourite dishes. My mother-in-law chided him gently, reminding him that she too had learned cooking slowly, refining her skills in time. She always stood by me, assuring me I would learn everything and that he needed to be patient.

"I agree, cooking was never my hobby. My mother had taught me the basics, and my father always praised whatever I made. I was a confident young woman, good at studies and sports, and I loved reading and writing. But gradually, I changed into someone submissive, always trying to please everyone around me, even at the cost of my own interests and identity.

"After my in-laws left for their native place, everything went downhill. I was left alone with a partner who seemed dissatisfied with everything I did. I tried my best to please him, but nothing was enough. Being a simple and naive girl, raised in a secure home and shielded from the harsher realities of life, I often felt disillusioned and depressed.

"Girls in our country are taught to adjust to every circumstance, especially in marriage. I tried my best to live up to that expectation. Even my mother advised me to keep quiet, do whatever my husband liked, and never show resentment."

Her eyes darkened as she continued, "It was later I came to know the truth. Sumit had been in love with a girl in college, someone full of life and flamboyance, admired by many. She rejected him for a better match and went abroad with her dream man. She even invited him to her wedding. It was his bruised ego that made him press his parents to arrange his own marriage quickly, before hers. And so, my marriage was solemnised in a hurry, to the surprised delight of my parents."

"You were his childhood friend. Did you know all this?" she asked me.

"No, I had no inkling of it," I replied.

At that moment I recalled why he had once said seriously that he now understood the meaning of *kisi ko mukammal jahan nahi milta.*

"So, what happened after that? Did you walk out as soon as you learned this truth?" I asked.

"Oh no," she sighed. "You know such things are not given much importance in our society. After all, it was in the past and considered over. Everyone around me said only the present mattered. But Sumit grew increasingly bitter. He criticized my taste in clothes, in makeup, in everything. He often compared me with the wives of his friends who were well dressed, smart, and more skilled in cooking. Slowly I began slipping into depression, losing interest in everything. Even my own reflection in the mirror seemed strange to me. I was turning into a ghost of myself."

She paused, her eyes distant, then continued. "Then one incident shook me to the core and changed the course of my life. A good friend of Sumit, who also loved books, gave me a few to read, knowing my interest in literature. He was a decent man, and I occasionally interacted with him, always in Sumit's presence. One day he came to ask for his books back. I invited him to sit and made tea. After a while, he left. At that very moment Sumit entered and saw the books and the teacups. His expression changed instantly.

"'So, you entertained him with tea even in my absence? I always noticed your special preference for him. He must be coming often, isn't it?' he accused.

"I was shell-shocked. How low could this man stoop? He gazed at me with disdain. And suddenly, the old Dharitri woke up inside me. I looked straight into his eyes and said, 'It is beneath my dignity to answer your question, and beneath my dignity to stay with you under the same roof. I am leaving. I hope you live in peace thereafter.'

"He was stunned by my outburst. Without a word, he went into the bedroom. I collected my belongings without a second thought. As I advanced toward the door, he shouted, 'Okay, go, but don't blame me. You are going on your own.'

"I looked back once and said, 'I thank you for helping me find my lost esteem. Best of luck to you.'"

I listened in silence, then asked, "What happened after that? How did you handle your life?"

"You come to my home tomorrow and have lunch with us," she said with a gentle smile. She asked where I was staying and promised to send her car with a driver the next day.

That night I could not sleep well. My dreams carried me back to school life, to the campus days, and Sumit too—though only as a schoolmate. The latter part of our lives was absent from the dream.

The next day I reached her home. It was a cozy and warm apartment. She welcomed me with affection and introduced me to a kind, gentle lady whom she addressed as "Ma."

"Your mother?" I asked softly.

The lady replied with a smile, "Yes, I am her mother and Rajiv's mother too. Please make yourself comfortable. I will set the table for lunch."

"My mother-in-law," Dharitri explained with affection, "but not less than a mother to me."

She resumed her story from where she had left it the previous afternoon. "After the incident, I went back to my parents' house. They were shocked and unhappy. To them, I had acted hastily. Such small quarrels, they said, were not unusual in married life. They worried about what the neighbours would think if I stayed away for too long. They tried to persuade me to return, but I had made up my mind. I refused and said I would rather die than be forced to go back.

"My elder brother stood by me. Just two years older, he was my friend and confidant. He suggested that I move into a hostel in town and told our parents that I would continue my research—the work I had given up because of the marriage. And so I came here, picked up the thread of my life, and tried to put the past behind me as if it were a nightmare."

She paused, then continued with a calm smile. "I used to come to the central library to collect research material. Rajiv, who had just joined as a librarian, helped me a great deal. Three years passed this way. I was ready with my thesis and went to thank all the library staff, including Rajiv, before bidding them farewell.

"I had been so absorbed in my work that the rest of the world had ceased to exist for me. When I stepped outside the library that day, I felt someone was following me. Rajiv proposed to me then, hesitantly and stammering, saying that if I did not agree it was all right; we could remain friends. It was a complete surprise for me. For the first time, I really noticed his large, deep eyes.

"I told him he did not even know me or my past, so how could he suddenly make such a proposal? He said he already knew everything about me through my brother and had been waiting for the right moment, because he did not want to lose me.

"I was not ready to take the plunge. Once bitten, twice shy. But my brother convinced me, stressing that this man was not like Sumit. He genuinely loved me. My brother, half jokingly and half seriously, even told me that Rajiv knew I was not a great cook and had little interest in jewelry or makeup. My parents were relieved, and a simple court marriage was arranged."

"So how is life now?" I asked.

"It is more than I ever expected," she replied with a gentle smile. "My life partner is loving and caring, and he tells me to be myself. My mother-in-law is even more loving than my own mother, so I feel blessed at last."

I rose to leave and asked if she had any news about my childhood buddy.

"He is in the same town," she said. "I heard he married a beautiful, lively woman soon after our divorce. I hope he finally found someone of his choice."

I asked for his address and left. That evening I decided to pay him a surprise visit.

Sumit was pleasantly surprised to see me. Age had given him a mature look and added some weight. What struck me most, though, was the loss of the sparkle and mischief in his eyes. We reminisced about our school days, and then I asked to meet his wife. Suddenly, he looked uncomfortable. Before he could speak, I said, "I know about the failure of your first marriage. I still want to meet your beautiful wife."

"She has gone to a picnic with my two children and her group of friends," he said.

"Without you? Why didn't you accompany them?" I asked.

"Come on," he replied, "why should I follow her everywhere? I have a backlog of work, and now I can complete it in peace."

Our eyes met. For all our past arguments, we had always been able to read each other.

"Perhaps I was wrong in my opinion about women," he sighed at last. "I had defined roles for them in my mind, like my mother, who did all the housework with calm and dignity, taking care of everyone without ever demanding anything."

"Do you think she was happy?" I asked quietly.

"What do you mean?" he said defensively.

"She never said she wanted something because you or your father never asked," I replied. "It was not your fault, Sumit. Women of that generation were brought up to think only of others and never of themselves. Their minds were wired that way."

"My mother told you she was not happy?" he asked, startled.

"No, of course not. How could she?" I said softly. "But you remember when mobile phones first came into the market? You and your father each had one. Your mother did not, because both of you thought it unnecessary since there was a landline at home. I still remember one day aunty asked me if she could make a call from my mobile. My first question was whether the landline was not working. She said it was working, but your father had told her to use it minimally so the bill would not be high. I still remember the wistful look in her eyes."

"Why didn't you tell me?" Sumit asked after a pause.

"Because I was young," I admitted. "And I felt it would sound like I was complaining about her.

"But now I want to tell you this — women are individuals, much more than just cooks or housekeepers. They have minds of their own, and they, too, long for genuine reciprocation of emotions and sentiments."

There was a long silence before he finally spoke, slowly and with regret.

"I realize now how vain I was. When I chose my second partner, I only thought of what I wanted. She is beautiful, an excellent cook, a wonderful host who organizes parties flawlessly; but I overlooked the subtlety, the quiet depth, that my mother and Dharitri carried within them. Because of her background, that refinement is missing. Everything appears perfect on the surface, yet an emptiness lingers with me. A loneliness I cannot escape.

"I feel guilty for what I did to Dharitri, and I cannot bring myself to face her. I only hope that, in her heart, she has forgiven me.
"She has," I said, "and she has found happiness with someone also."

"You are in touch with her?" he said in a surprised tone.

"Met her two days back and got your address from her only."

"Does she remember me?" he asked slowly.

"You are a past chapter in her life; there is no rancor, and no emotions attached."

Did I find a lost look in those eyes? Perhaps.

I got up to leave. "Keep in touch please," he said.

"Yes, Sure… *kabhi zameen kabhi aasman nahi milta,"* I said, and we both smiled.

COMPLETE BY MYSELF

I overslept that day, perhaps because of the hectic schedule of the previous one. When I woke up, the television had already been switched on, and the local news was playing. Slightly irritated, I walked over to turn it off, but the anchor's voice stopped me midway.

The newsreader announced that the leading businesswoman, owner of the famous Teddy Shop, Beena Kedia, had passed away the previous night. Though the cause of death was not yet confirmed, it appeared she had suffered a heart attack.

I was startled. How could she be gone so suddenly? I mentally calculated her age; she must have been sixty or sixty-one. With her good health and never-say-die spirit, it did not seem an age to leave this world.

I immediately called Ruma to know more. With a subdued voice she said the family had learned of the tragedy from the same news channel and had gathered at her residence to make arrangements. She asked me to join her in this moment of grief.

By the time I reached, a crowd had gathered, and reporters were busy with their cameras. Ruma came forward, embraced me, and her swollen eyes brimmed with tears. My own eyes misted as I held her close. She had lost her mother, and I had lost a dear aunt—a woman of pure soul. I touched the feet of my now-departed aunt and sat quietly in a corner. Among the crowd, I saw Ruma's father, her younger sister Soma, and her youngest brother Somesh with his wife. The whole family had come together to mourn the death of the woman who had long ago chosen her own path, leaving her family behind.

Her father, seeing me, said in an anguished voice that despite repeated attempts his wife had refused to return. I felt a hollow inside. His sorrow seemed almost superficial.

Ruma and I had been school classmates and very close. Most of us came from humble middle-class backgrounds, but Ruma's family was affluent, running a steady business. At that age, our parents took pride in teaching us honesty, uprightness, and self-respect. Wealth did not influence us much, though we did enjoy it when she came in her car to take a few of us to spend Sundays at her home. The big haveli, with many servants and delicious lunches, always made our day. With one younger sister and a brother, the family seemed happy-go-lucky in our eyes.

In those days we believed only what we saw. We never looked deeper into life's meanings, or the sermons elders gave from time to time. So, when Ruma was absent for a month, we were curious but not overly worried. Long absences for family functions were not unusual.

When she returned, we gathered around her for gossip but were taken aback when she said her mother had been unwell, and the family had gone abroad for treatment. Beena auntie, as we called her, had always appeared a quiet, sober, and smiling woman. She did not join in our teenage chatter but watched us with fondness. A dedicated housewife and loving mother, she also had a talent for making beautiful stuffed toys, especially teddy bears.

I once told her she could earn a fortune selling them. She laughed it off, saying it was only a hobby. "But auntie, what will you do with so many toys?" I asked. She smiled, handed me a little pink doll with sparkling eyes, and said she loved giving them away to children who wanted them. That was all.

Later, when alone with Ruma, I asked what had happened. "My mother suffered from severe depression," she said quietly. "That's why we went abroad. Hopefully, she is all right now." At the time, the word "depression" was not common, and I hardly thought more about it.

After finishing school, Ruma and I joined the same college. We enjoyed the transition from adolescence to youth but eventually went our separate ways, promising to keep in touch. Life soon became busy with family, children, and responsibilities. Communication with old friends faded.

One day Ruma called and asked me to meet her. Delighted, I agreed. When we met, I noticed a sadness in her eyes. On asking, she revealed her mother had left home and was living alone in a single rented room on the other side of town.

At first, I could not imagine such a docile and obedient woman taking such a drastic step. "But why?" I asked.

Ruma sighed. "My brother fell in love with a girl from a Scheduled Caste. Despite my mother's strong protests, he married her. My father was too absorbed in his business to interfere. We sisters were already married. My mother said either she would stay in the house or her son with his wife. My brother thought she was only threatening and brought his bride home. The next day, my mother moved out."

I asked gently, "Tell me one thing, Ruma. Why did your mother go into depression when everything looked so perfect to us?"

She was quiet, then said, "There were many reasons, which I found out later. One of the biggest was my father's affair. When my younger sister was born, a nurse was hired to help my mother, who was very ill. The nurse was young and attractive. My father, who deep down resented my mother's plain looks and lack of education, easily fell for her. My poor mother had no choice but to suffer silently."

"Oh, that must have been hard for auntie. What was the outcome?" I asked.

"My grandmother took a strong stand, not so much for my mother as out of fear of losing her command over the family. The nurse was dismissed, and slowly things returned to normal, but the wound in my mother's heart never healed. That, along with countless restrictions, took its toll. Signs of depression appeared years later."

We sat silently for some time, lost in our thoughts. Strange how tragedies unfold in the lives of those close to us yet go unnoticed.

I said softly, "Perhaps auntie's disappointment grew because she relied on her children after being let down elsewhere. She could not accept her son's step."

"Perhaps," Ruma agreed. "But don't you think she could have avoided such an extreme step? I did try to talk to her. I was living with my in-laws when I first heard of it. By the time I visited, she had made up her mind. She refused to move back home or even with me. She said she would never create disturbance in my life."

I asked, "How did she manage expenses?"

Ruma smiled faintly. "Do you remember her hobby?"

"Of course. Those lovely stuffed toys, especially teddy bears of all sizes," I said.

"Yes, but you also remember she never wanted to turn it into a profession," Ruma replied. "Once our rooms were half-filled with them. My father threatened to throw them out. But her friend, who had already taken up the craft as a business, encouraged her. She suggested dividing the toys—half to be donated to orphanages and half to be sold. With the proceeds, she could buy raw material. She even convinced my mother to open a bank account. None of us knew then how important that step would become."

"Destiny has its own way," I murmured.

"Will auntie meet me if I go to her place?

"No, now is not the right time. Let some time pass," my friend said. I returned with a heavy heart; with time I almost forgot this conversation.

Years passed. Then one day, while shopping, I noticed a store with a teddy bear sign. The neon nameplate read *Teddy Bear*. Curious, I entered. Inside were rows of beautiful stuffed toys, each smiling at the world.

When I asked for the owner, the salesgirl pointed to a corner. At first, I did not recognize her, but as I moved closer, my heart leapt. It was Beena auntie. She had aged but gracefully. She radiated self-confidence and carried herself with quiet pride. When she recognized me, she clasped my hand with joy.

"What a pleasant surprise!" she exclaimed.

I was too full of emotion to reply. She took me upstairs to a well-furnished little room and made me sit. After some time, I asked how she was.

"You tell me," she said with a twinkle in her eyes. "How do I look?"

Before I could answer, she added, "I am content with my life. I am complete by myself."

"Auntie, what made you take such a step, leaving everything behind?" I asked gently.

"It was not sudden," she said after a pause. "Yes, a trigger came, and then things happened."

I pleaded for details. She grew silent for a while, her eyes far away, then spoke simply. "I was brought up in a traditional family where girls were instilled with values and principles from a young age. In those days, moral lectures were only for women. Men were never taught how to adjust or sacrifice. It was the woman's duty to hold the family together through sacrifice, selfless love, and loyalty.

"It may sound strange to your generation, but in my time, girls were told that if a man strayed, it was the woman's fault. She had failed to charm him, failed to hold him with her beauty and devotion. That is why mothers taught their daughters *solah shringar and triyacharitra* as essential traits."

She gave a faint smile. "I silently rebelled against such ideas, but I had no courage to voice them. I was not beautiful, but I was good at studies and handcrafts. After matriculation, I wanted to study further, but my elders said my education was enough. They feared college would spoil me. That was the first major sacrifice.

"My marriage became the priority. My parents felt fortunate to find a groom from a good business family. Never mind the huge dowry required for an ordinary-looking girl like me. So I was married at seventeen, burdened with instructions and expectations. My first child came soon, and two years later another, both daughters. Everyone pressed for a son. At last, when my third child, my first son, was born, the family rejoiced."

Auntie stopped and was quiet for a long time. Then she asked me directly, "You knew about my treatment for depression, didn't you?"

"I did," I admitted softly.

Ruma had once confided in me, trying to explain the long absence from school.

She didn't beat around the bush; instead, she looked at me directly and said, "You must already know the real reason." My silence was enough of an answer. She didn't press further but admitted that it had been one of the darkest, most difficult phases of her life. Though she carried herself with calm and dignity at the time, the scars showed themselves years later.

I asked her why she hadn't confronted her husband then and there. A faint, wry smile appeared on her face. "Haven't I already told you about my upbringing? In our world, if such things happened, the woman was always blamed. With so little education, and no one to stand by me, where could I have gone?"

Her voice quivered as she continued. She told me how her husband never missed an opportunity to belittle her, to remind her of her "ordinary" looks and her lack of polished conversation. At social gatherings, he would compare her, almost mockingly, to the wives of his colleagues, who spoke English with effortless fluency, while she could barely manage a few simple sentences. For him, her skills as a homemaker held no value.

At one point, she fixed her eyes on mine, her gaze raw with hurt. "Can you imagine," she asked softly, "the pain of having your self-esteem chipped away, your confidence crushed—again and again—by someone you cannot walk away from?"

I had no words. I simply held her hand in silence, letting her know I was there. After a while, she composed herself, and with quiet strength she said, "What kept me going were my children. Their love was unconditional. It was their support that made me strong, that gave me the resilience to survive."

After handing me my cup of tea, Auntie sat quietly, sipping hers in complete silence. I could feel the weight of unspoken words between us and braced myself for the question that had been on my mind for so long. Finally, I asked, "You loved your children so deeply. How could one act from one of them push you so far as to abandon them? After being such a supportive parent all along, couldn't you forgive?"

She paused for a long moment, staring into the distance. Then she said softly, "Do you really think my son marrying against my wishes was the only reason I left everything behind?"

Her words confused me. "That was the reason as far as I know," I said.

"Yes," she replied, "I was shocked by his decision. The stigma in society was hard to face. But if only my son had put his arms around me, asked for my forgiveness, told me he loved me and knew my love for him was strong enough to forgive—then I would have accepted everything with an open heart."

Her eyes dimmed as she continued. "What cut deepest was not his marriage. It was the way he changed. He became his father, telling me he now understood how his father felt about my lack of education and my inability to 'keep up with the times.' He said his wife was highly qualified and that he would always feel proud to accompany her, unlike the discomfort his father had felt with me."

Auntie's voice trembled. "I was stunned by his outburst. The smug expression on his father's face added salt to the wound. Tears rolled down my cheeks that night as I cried harder than I ever had before. My self-respect had been attacked beyond repair, and years of silent sacrifice rose before me. That was the moment something inside me detached. By morning, my mind had decided. I left that house—the house that was supposed to be my home. I never turned back, and I have never regretted it."

I hesitated before asking, "But didn't you feel insecure, starting out on your own?"

Her expression grew calm. "At that time, I was devoid of all feelings. Later, with the help of a true friend who stood by me like a rock, I started a small venture. My husband and son were furious. They threatened to disown me, to cut me off from any share of property. But I had already gone beyond all of that. I told them to do as they pleased. For me, that chapter of my life was closed."

She straightened a little as she spoke of what came after. "Those first days were hard. There were awkward questions, jeers, and whispers. But I remained unfazed. I had nothing to lose, and that gave me a strange sense of freedom. Slowly, I rebuilt myself, not just as a homemaker, but as a woman with a mind of her own. It's ironic. Women of my time rarely thought of their own identity. We were always someone's daughter, someone's wife, someone's sister or mother. And if we dared think of ourselves as individuals, there were always plenty of people ready to make us feel guilty about it."

Before I left, I asked if she had reconnected with her family. She smiled faintly. "After overcoming my shortcomings and making a life of my own, I began attending a few gatherings I was invited to. At one such event, I was asked to deliver a motivational speech to poor women who felt left behind. I spoke in both English and Hindi, answering their questions. And then I noticed my husband in the audience, staring at me with disbelief. Perhaps it was beyond his imagination that his wife could transform like this after leaving him."

She gave a small laugh. "A month later, he called me. He said, 'Let bygones be bygones. Come back.'" She turned to me and asked quietly, "What would you have done in my place?"

"What you did, Auntie," I said softly.

She looked serene. "I declined. I couldn't fit back into the same groove again. But I hold no bitterness for anyone now. I see it as a blessing in disguise. God gave me the chance to live as a woman who stood upright after stumbling and survived on her own."

When I rose to leave, she held my hand. "When I'm gone," she whispered, "tell my children that I loved them always, and that they should never regret what happened."

I tried to smile. "Auntie, you'll live long. We'll meet again."

But that turned out to be our last meeting. When I went to attend her final rites, I passed on her message to her children. And in their eyes, for a fleeting moment, I thought I saw relief, a burden of unspoken love finally lifted.

ATTACHED IN AN UNATTACHED WAY

It was never easy for her, right from the beginning, life had tested her. Born into a middle-class family as the third daughter, her arrival was seen not as a blessing but almost as a curse. Her parents, weary of societal whispers and burdened by expectations, had prayed fervently for a son. When she came instead, the joy of birth was replaced by disappointment, not just for her parents but for the entire extended family.

As a child, she was blissfully unaware of the disapproving glances and the indifferent treatment that shadowed her presence. But as she grew, she began to notice the subtle preferences, the dismissive tones, the way affection was unevenly distributed by parents and grandparents alike.

What kept her afloat through these silent storms was the bond she shared with her two sisters. Together, the three formed a fortress of love and understanding. Every joy, every wound, every secret found its way into their small circle. When one faltered, the others consoled; when one rejoiced, the others celebrated.

All three girls attended a nearby school. Bright, diligent, and full of promise, they excelled in academics and extracurriculars. Teachers adored them, classmates admired them. Yet, the moment they stepped back into their home, the warmth of school life evaporated. Within those walls, comparisons reigned. The eldest, blessed with beauty and being the firstborn, drew favor. The middle one was tolerated. And she, the youngest , was left to fill in the shadows.

By nature, she was calm, patient, and giving. She never complained about the disproportionate share of household chores she shouldered. She never demanded, never rebelled, and accepted whatever little came her way. But deep within, a dream had taken root. A fragile, closely guarded dream: to stand tall one day as an independent woman, to earn respect on her own terms, to be someone impossible to overlook. She kept this dream locked within her heart, never daring to share it even with her sisters, for fear they might laugh at its audacity.

Time moved on. By the time she finished school, her two elder sisters were married off, their lives diverted into new households. And she, still standing quietly at the threshold of her own journey, held on to her secret dream, waiting for the day it could finally breathe.

Her mother would often lament that nothing was left for her, worrying aloud about what future awaited this quiet, dutiful daughter. Those words left their mark, and she resolved to carve her own path. She began giving tuitions to younger students from her school, and with every rupee she saved, she inched closer to her first step of independence—a diploma in education. Soon after, she found a teaching job. Her days were filled with classrooms, her evenings with tuition sessions. Life settled into a steady, uneventful rhythm. Yet, there was a subtle shift: she was no longer dismissed or pitied. Earning brought her respect, and she realized a hard truth—money had the power to change the way the world looked at her.

Time, that old gypsy man, never lingers for anyone. It carried her steadily into her thirties. When a marriage proposal finally arrived, her family hesitated. After all, her steady income had become their comfort. But whispers from neighbors grew louder, and appearances had to be maintained. At last, they agreed.

Her new family was small—just her husband, who ran a modest store, and her mother-in-law. To her relief, her in-laws had no objection to her working. In fact, her teaching job was one of the reasons the proposal had been so appealing. She adapted quickly, balancing her responsibilities at home with her school duties.

Then came a turning point, pregnancy. It stirred something long buried within her. She remembered her childhood dream of standing tall on her own, commanding respect. But now, she folded that dream into her unborn child. She vowed that her child would receive everything she had once been denied—love, opportunity, dignity.

When her son was born, she felt, for the first time, whole. A surge of fulfillment filled the empty spaces of her life. He became her sun, her reason, her world. She poured into him the affection and comfort she had hungered for as a child. The entire family adored him, and in his smile, she discovered a new meaning to life.

From his earliest years, she began shaping his path. He was bright, brimming with energy and charm, and she found immense joy in watching him blossom. She personally guided his studies, and he rewarded her faith with success after success. By the time he finished school, he had earned a place in the best college of the region. An all-rounder, gifted in academics, sports, and extra-curriculars—he embodied everything she had once dreamed of being. His achievements felt like her own.

Her world had grown small; the outside no longer mattered. All that counted was his growth, his future. So, when he won a scholarship for higher studies in the United States, her heart wavered. Rationally, she knew she must support him, must cheer him on with pride. But deep inside, the thought of distance gnawed at her. She was torn between joy and grief.

Her son, wise beyond his years, sensed her turmoil. He promised her he would return as soon as his studies were complete and reassured her that he would never settle abroad. His words soothed her, even if they could not erase her dread of parting.

The final day arrived. The entire family accompanied him to the station, each step heavy with unspoken emotion. For her, it felt as though the axis of her world was shifting, her heart being tugged in two directions—one towards hope, the other towards loss.

Life suddenly felt hollow. The house echoed with silence, and she moved through her days as though a part of her had withered away. Nothing seemed to hold meaning anymore, yet she carried on with her teaching job, the only anchor that gave her solace. Modern technology softened the distance somewhat; her son would call or write regularly, and hearing his voice or reading his words brought her a fragile comfort. She clung to his progress as though it were her own heartbeat.

Then came the news. With his brilliant record, he had been offered a job the moment he completed his project work. “It’s a lifetime chance,” he said. She felt her chest tighten. This was the first real shock. She longed to remind him of his promise to return, of the assurance he had given her, but she bit her tongue. Her husband, though generally uninvolved in career matters, expressed disapproval. Even her mother-in-law voiced her unease, warning that he might marry a firangi and settle down permanently in foreign lands. “It was unwise,” she said, “to let him go so far without a rope to pull him back.”

But she was not one for arguments. She stayed silent, burying her turmoil in routine. School, tuitions, housework, her body moved through the motions while her mind wavered between hope and dread. She told herself she was close to retirement, that after next year she would finally rest, perhaps even pursue hobbies long abandoned. Yet, beneath that calm surface, the thought clawed at her relentlessly: What if he never returns? What if all she had lived for slips away? Every dream, every sacrifice had been tied to one vision, her son’s success and their life together. The thought of that vision breaking apart rattled her soul.

And then, one morning, the blow fell. She opened her email as usual, but this time her eyes froze on the screen. Just three lines, so brief, yet sharp enough to shatter the world she had built brick by brick with sacrifices no one else had seen.

"Ma, I have got a promising job. I have decided to stay here, so forgive me. The most important news is that I have found my soul-mate who belongs to this country and doesn't want to leave."

The words blurred. Her mind raced so fast that she could no longer make sense of them. Her worst fear, her unspoken apprehension, had come true. For a moment, she sat in stunned silence, unable to move, unable to think.

By the time she regained some composure, her husband had already left for the store, and her mother-in-law was out gossiping with her circle of old companions. A small wave of relief washed over her; she wasn't ready to face anyone yet. She slipped back into her routine, keeping her hands busy while her heart drowned in turmoil. No one noticed any change; her discipline had always been her armor. But inside, she was breaking.

Where had she gone wrong? The question gnawed at her. Had there been something lacking in her upbringing? Should she have instilled in him a stronger love for his country? She searched her memories, but nowhere could she recall encouraging him to leave. She had only ever wanted to see him thrive. And yet, in that moment, it felt as though her life's purpose had betrayed her.

It took her fifteen days to settle down mentally. People face great tragedies and survive, and this was in no way a tragedy in the eyes of the world. Finally, she revealed the news to her husband and mother-in-law. She had braced herself to face the dismay and disappointment on their faces. Her mother-in-law was vocal about her displeasure, blaming her for the leverage she had given to her son which had led to this stage. Her husband did not speak much except to say that he had been thinking of going on a pilgrimage with the family once their son returned, but now it seemed meaningless.

After the conversation, she thought deeply about her life. She had compromised all along, adjusted with every situation that came her way, and forgotten herself once she became a mother. Her own desires and wishes had been pushed to the background. She had shifted her dream onto that small child who once looked up at her with complete trust and love. She had vowed to raise him in the best possible way, to give him every opportunity so that he could blossom into a wonderful human being spreading warmth all around. Had she failed? Her mind replied firmly, No. She had succeeded.

Still, she could not ignore a long-forgotten dream from her childhood—the dream of standing on her own and commanding respect from everyone around her. True, she had stood on her own, but in the process, she had lost her identity. She had been a daughter, then a wife, a daughter-in-law, and finally a mother. But who was she as a person? What were her strengths and weaknesses, and how much had she ever worked on herself? Now she decided the time had come to rediscover her own self and fulfill her childhood dream.

She began to plan her post-retirement life. No more sitting at home, cooling her heels. A new phase had to begin. At her farewell party, colleagues who had become like family wished her well and even offered suggestions. The principal praised her sincerity and dedication and expressed hope that she would remain a guiding force for the school. She felt nostalgic. Often, we take things for granted only to realize their worth after losing them.

After a short pause, she began working on her plan. She rented a house nearby and obtained a license to open an academy for school children. She named it 'Bud to Flower Academy'. Some of her colleagues found the name unusual, but she explained that it was self-explanatory: here, young minds—the buds—would be given a chance to bloom into flowers. At first, parents from the neighborhood approached her. She explained her mission, and ten children joined her first batch. They belonged to different classes and had difficulties in different subjects. She allotted them separate timings after school and on weekends. Two of her retired colleagues soon joined her, and the academy began to grow.

The motto was simple: no harsh words, no punishment. Children who struggled were treated with patience. Throughout her teaching career, she had believed in all-round development and had discovered that every child carried a unique quality. Such qualities, she believed, should be nurtured. So, besides coaching in subjects, she helped each child develop what they loved most. The most interesting outcome was that children who lagged in studies, once praised and encouraged for their special qualities, gradually improved in academics as well. Understanding and encouragement worked wonders, and slowly, the buds began to bloom into flowers.

Within a year, the number of students grew so much that she had to rent a double-story building. More retired colleagues joined, and together they ran the academy, sharing benefits equally. Her dream had finally become a reality. She now commanded the respect she had yearned for all her life. Life had indeed opened a new door after closing one, and she rose again with renewed strength. Money was no longer a problem, but the respect in the eyes of her students and their parents was her true treasure.

At this time, her mother-in-law's failing health reminded her of a long-standing wish: *The Char Dham Yatra.* She decided to take a break and arranged for the pilgrimage. Her partners promised to manage the academy in her absence. Her son, now a father himself, would call her often. Her daughter-in-law too spoke to her frequently, and a bond had developed between them. She felt happy for their progress. Having developed the strength of no-expectation, she harbored no resentment in her heart.

A few days before the pilgrimage, while returning from the academy, she saw a small crowd gathered outside her house. Fear gripped her as she rushed forward, only to find herself face to face with her son. She froze. For a moment, she could only stare, stunned. God, he was standing before her in flesh and blood, looking so handsome. Emotions long buried surged back, and tears flowed freely as he embraced her tightly.

When she regained herself, she asked why he was standing outside. He explained that his grandmother had shut the door, refusing to let his foreign wife inside. Years ago, she might have reacted differently, but time and experience had changed her. She looked closely at the woman she had once silently blamed for taking her son away. Her eyes revealed hesitation and a hint of fear, but not hostility. In her arms was a cute toddler clinging tightly to his mother.

She stepped forward, looked straight into her daughter-in-law's eyes, and said softly, "I longed for a daughter so much, and now I have one." The young woman's expression changed, and with moist eyes, she stepped willingly into her arms. Taking her grandson, she opened the side door with her own key and motioned them to follow. She placed the little boy on her mother-in-law's lap. The old woman was bewildered, but children don't wait for responses. The toddler leaned forward and kissed his great-grandmother on the cheek. In that moment, all inhibitions melted, and the old woman clung to him, crying with joy.

When her husband returned that evening, he looked more relaxed and content than he had in years. On the fourth day of his visit, her son disclosed the reason for his sudden arrival. He confessed that he had planned to call first but decided to come in person. Holding her hands and looking pleadingly at his father, he said he wanted them all to come and stay with him in the United States. He had acquired citizenship, bought a home with every comfort, and did not want his aging parents and grandmother to live so far away.

A heavy silence filled the room. Sometimes silence speaks louder than words. What should they do? Leave everything behind and spend their days basking in the love of family, or remain rooted where they belonged? She looked at her husband and saw the uncertainty in his eyes. She knew her mother-in-law would hardly survive in a foreign land. She herself had turned her dream into reality and was enjoying the twilight of her life.

That night, she discussed it with her husband and mother-in-law. Together, they decided what was best for everyone. In the morning, she spoke to her son. "Son, we are like old trees now. If uprooted, we will not survive for long. It is better we stay where our roots are. It would be selfish to ask you to return after everything you have built with your hard work. Promise us only that you will visit once or twice a year if possible. We are happy to see you happy, and in the end, that is all that matters."

Once the decision was made, she felt calm and at peace. She had discovered the power of detachment. Remaining attached in an unattached way gave her a quiet strength and a deep faith that everything would be taken care of by the Almighty to whom she had surrendered completely.

ME TIME

"Hello auntie, can I meet you for some time today?"

It was the voice of the son of one of my closest friends. I asked him if everything was alright. He assured me it was, but repeated his request with an urgency that made me pause. When I invited him for lunch, he quickly refused, asking instead if we could meet somewhere outside the home where he could speak freely. Intrigued, I suggested a nearby coffee house at noon. He readily agreed.

I had known him since the day he was born. Children usually opened up to me easily, for I loved their company. I presumed he wanted some career advice, though he was already doing well in a good job and appeared quite content.

When we met, he was hesitant at first, fumbling for words. But after a while, he finally blurted it out. "It's about mom. I wanted to talk to you about her."

"Is Ruchi unwell? Something serious?" I asked, alarmed.

"No, auntie, she is fine."

"Then what is it? Tell me."

He looked down for a moment and then spoke slowly. "Mom has decided to go alone on a long journey."

I stared at him, baffled.

"The destination is unknown," he added quickly, "because she refuses to share where she is going. The whole family is worried. I was hoping you could talk to her, auntie. Maybe convince her not to do this."

I promised I would visit her the next day and returned home, troubled by his words.

Memories came rushing back. We had a lively girl gang during our school days, and Ruchi was our leader. Jovial, outspoken, bold, she was the one full of life among us. I still remember the day when our English teacher, irritated, ordered her out of the classroom. She walked out without protest, wandered around for a while, and then strolled back in, asking with mock innocence, "May I come in, sir?" The whole class burst out laughing, and even sir could not hide his smile as he allowed her in. That was Ruchi, fearless and lighthearted.

She was never the topper but always among the top five. School life with her was full of fun, playing pranks on boys, doing mimicry of teachers, laughing till our sides hurt. How much I still missed those carefree days.

Though we chose different colleges, we stayed in touch. Later, both of us settled in the same town. Ruchi seemed to have it all, a successful businessman for a husband, two lovely children, and a life that made her look like the very picture of the happily married ever after tale we all admired.

And now this. Where did she want to go at this stage of life, when most of us were ready to hang our boots and finally slow down?

The next day I went to her home. She looked surprised to see me, but I was even more surprised to see her, bags packed and ready.

"So?" I asked.

"All my bags are packed, I'm ready to go," she sang with a mischievous smile, recalling the song we once hummed together in school.

"Yes, I'm ready to go," she said more firmly. "Wish me luck."

"But where, and why?" I asked, still confused.

"Where I haven't decided. And why, because I have a strong urge to do so." She looked at me, calm and determined.

I could see that wandering look in her eyes, that longing to be free of all bondage.

"But why all of a sudden, Ruchi?" I asked.

"It is not all of a sudden. It has been shaping in my thoughts for a long time," she replied calmly.

"Fine… but why alone? Won't you feel lonely?" I pressed.

A haunted look returned to her eyes. "Was I never lonely before?" she asked softly. "After a few years of marriage my husband immersed himself in business, always traveling, while I managed everything with two growing kids on my own. Was I not lonely then? When the children grew up and built their own lives, was I not alone again? I was always someone to attend to everyone's needs, just that. Tell me, was I not lonely then?"

She paused, then added, "Look, I am not complaining. I am glad my children are settled, and my husband is among the top businessmen of the town. But don't you think I deserve a bit of 'me time' now? And as for going alone, who should I ask to accompany me? Don't you see it would become a compulsion for them? And that is something I never want."

In that moment I glimpsed again the fearless, carefree friend I had known in school.

"Wait for one year," I teased, "I'll accompany you."

She laughed heartily. "Why wait? I am not going to perish. We'll take another trip together next year."

When I stepped out, I patted her son on the shoulder and said gently, "Let your mom be. Don't worry, she is a strong woman and can take care of herself. She will be back—she isn't planning to settle in the Himalayas. And even if she does," I added with a smile, "let her be. She has given the best years of her life to all of you, and now she deserves some time for herself."

ONLY FEELINGS, NO NAME

"Mother is serious, the doctors have almost given up," my brother called up to inform.

He further said, he was taking her home as *ma* said she did not want to die in the hospital.

I felt numb. In a jiffy, I decided to visit her. My tickets were booked, it was a break journey as there was no direct train connectivity. The journey was long, and I wanted to reach as soon as possible. Next day after a brief stopover when I boarded the next train, I was full of apprehensions, suppose I couldn't reach in time? I prayed to God for her wellbeing, though mother was in her seventies, the thought of losing her never crossed my mind. We were a big family – altogether eight brothers and sisters; father was strict and a man of few words, but *ma* was full of love and care. She was a friend in which we all confided everything.

Time had taken its toll on her, all my siblings were married and well settled. The death of my father had made her a lonely figure. There were only a few occasions, when all her children gathered, and *ma* was her old self at such times. No body lives forever but some partings are tough to bear. "Excuse me", someone addressed me, breaking my chain of thoughts, I looked up to find a lady of almost my age.

"You see, the charging points are not working on our seats. Can I charge my mobile here if you don't mind?"

"Of course, I said. "Please sit."

There were three women on the other side, two of them were quiet, only third one was talkative.

Soon she became friendly with all, around her, finding me subdued she wanted to know the reason.

When I told her the purpose of my journey, she was quiet for some time and then said,

"Don't worry she will recover."

To change the subject, I asked her about her destination to which she replied they were a group on pilgrimage and were on way to visit a famous Shiva temple on Shivratri. She further told me they were Tamilians settled in Sri Lanka for long but migrated recently due to constant violence there. I fell silent after that and was lost in my thoughts.

"Do you think they are newly married couple or girlfriend and boyfriend?" I looked in the direction she was pointing. A young couple were sitting cozy, lost in each other, oblivious to the world around them. They hugged each other in between small talks.

"How do I know, and moreover it is none of my business," I said.

"Yes, I know it is none of our business, but don't you think they should show some restraint in public places."

I nodded as I was in no mood to argue.

Unable to keep quiet for long, she asked if I was a working woman, I said, yes. "I teach in a women's college." "Oh so lucky you are," she exclaimed, "you looked like a writer to me."

I was bit amused and said I do that also off and on, "But you are not going to find my name in any writers' column or while surfing the internet." She chuckled and said it hardly mattered.

"Tell me one thing, if you don't mind", she continued , "your mother must be quite old isn't it?" I understood what she meant, so I said yes. "She is old but so what? She has always been a pillar of strength for me… supportive and caring."

"I am slightly jealous of you, not all mothers are supportive and understanding," she said and "I don't mean stepmother here".

My questioning glance urged her to continue. She began softly, "I was a good student and had always dreamed of becoming a doctor, but my education was cut short after high school. We were not well off; my father managed a small business that barely kept us afloat. My mother decided it would be more practical for me to join stitching classes. She believed that learning such a skill would not only support the family but also increase my chances of finding a suitable match in the future.

"I hated the idea. I tried everything to dissuade her — hunger strikes, endless tantrums — but nothing worked. She was firm in her belief, and even my father couldn't intervene. My mother felt that once I acquired this skill, I could contribute to the family income and ensure my two younger brothers received a better education. I loved my brothers deeply, but giving up my dreams for their sake felt unbearable. My silent suffering created a distance between my mother and me, and slowly she became a stranger."

I now understood why she had said she was jealous. By then, she had my full attention. She continued, her eyes far away. "One day, while I sat silently crying in a corner of the terrace, I felt a pair of eyes on me. Startled, I looked up and saw a young man watching. Embarrassed, I quickly turned my face away, wondering who he was and what right he had to intrude upon my small refuge.

"Soon, we came to know he was the nephew of our neighbour and had come to spend his vacation here. I was vexed at first by this new intruder who seemed to invade my privacy.

"I began attending my stitching classes unwillingly. The classes were not very close, about a twenty-minute walk from home. One day, already running late, I decided to take a shortcut. The lane was deserted, eerily quiet, and no one was around.

"After a while, out of nowhere, two bikes carrying four men sped past me. Noticing I was alone, they turned back, circled around, and blocked my path, offering me a ride. The look in their eyes made my blood run cold. Terrified, I quickened my steps into a near run, trying to ignore them, but they followed persistently and almost cornered me. I cannot describe the panic that seized me in that moment. A flood of dreadful possibilities flashed through my mind. I pleaded with them to let me go, stammering that I was late, all the while praying silently to God for help.

"Emboldened by my fear, they pressed harder. 'Come on, we will drop you wherever you want,' they said with mocking confidence. And then, as if my desperate prayers had been heard, another bike screeched to a halt right beside me. A firm voice commanded, 'Sit behind.' Startled, I turned to see the neighbor's nephew, and without a moment's hesitation, I climbed on. Before the others could react, he sped away, leaving them behind.

"Once we reached the main road, he asked me where I wanted to go. Still dazed and with tears brimming in my eyes, I could only point to the building ahead. When he stopped, I finally looked up to thank him. For a brief moment, our eyes met, and my heart skipped a beat. There was something inexplicable in those large eyes, something that calmed and comforted me in a way I had never felt before.

"'Take care,' he said gently. 'These lanes are not safe when you're alone. Luckily, I happened to be there. Promise me you won't take such risks again.' His voice carried an authority that left no room for argument. Completely tongue-tied, I only nodded. In the next moment, he was gone."

By now, I was completely absorbed in her story and asked eagerly, "What happened after that?"

With a faraway look in her eyes, she smiled faintly. "If you are expecting a dramatic climax, I am sorry to disappoint you."

"Go on," I urged.

"After some time, when I had calmed down, I replayed the whole incident in my mind again and again. What surprised me most was that I had jumped onto his bike without a second thought. Why? He was also a stranger to me. Perhaps it was instinct, or perhaps it was God's way of sending me help. But what stayed with me even more than the rescue was the firmness in his voice, the way he made me promise not to repeat such mistakes, and that unfathomable look in his eyes. It was as if, without warning, some invisible bond had been formed between us.

"When I returned home, I was a changed person. Quiet, serene, almost radiant. No one noticed, of course, and I could not have confided in anyone even if I wanted to. But inside me, something had shifted. The roof corner once again became my favorite refuge, and sometimes, when our eyes met across that space, a brief smile or a small nod was all it took to make me feel alive.

"After a long time, I felt happy again. So complete that even my mother noticed. She remarked that perhaps I had finally understood how right she was in sending me to those stitching classes. I was too full to contradict her.

"That was the best phase of my life. Everything seemed so beautiful, every little detail brimming with warmth and love. At last, I understood what it truly meant to be sweet sixteen.

"I wanted to know everything about him, but I never had the courage to ask anyone directly. The little I managed to gather was that he was preparing for competitive exams after graduation.

That explained why he was always surrounded by books on the rooftop, soaking in the sunlight. Yet, in my heart, I felt there was another reason behind that sunlight, one only the two of us silently shared.

"Life went on with the same routine. If any change was happening within me, it remained invisible to the world around."

I could not resist interrupting her at this point. "So, was there any letter writing or secret meetings, like in the movies?" I asked, half curious and half amused.

She chuckled softly. "No, nothing of that sort ever happened."

Then her tone shifted. "One day, I noticed a sadness in his eyes while we sat in our respective roof corners. We looked at each other for a long time, and I felt a tug at my heart. Why was he sad? Just then his aunt came out, gently patted his shoulder, and spoke to him as if consoling him.

"Later that evening, I happened to meet his aunt in a shop. Unable to hold back, I asked casually, 'Auntie, who was the guest you were consoling on the roof? Was something serious?'

"Being a simple and unsuspecting woman, she was glad to find an interested listener. She told me that her nephew had come to stay for a few days after his exams and was busy preparing for competitive exams. That morning his graduation result had been declared. Always a topper, this time he had narrowly missed the top rank and had been feeling low. But by evening, she assured me, he was fine again.

"'Oh, only for that,' I blurted out in relief. Seeing her curious look, I quickly added, 'Of course I understand how disappointing it must be to miss a position so narrowly.'

"Pleased by my response, she went on, 'I was surprised to learn you discontinued your studies. I remember you winning many awards during school annual days. Parents used to be so proud.' Her son had been two years junior to me in school.

"Her words stirred an old pain I thought had long since faded. I quickly bid her goodbye and returned home.

"For the next few days, our family was away attending a close relative's wedding. I felt restless the whole time and could not enjoy the celebrations. Many people kept asking about me, and what irritated me most was my mother's repeated tale about her plans to find me a suitable match.

"As soon as we returned, I rushed to my favorite roof corner, only to feel disappointed when I did not see the one I longed for. The next day, however, we were face to face again. Relief washed over both of us. Strange how words were unnecessary. The mere presence of each other, even from a distance, was enough.

"Almost three months had passed. My training was about to end when, one afternoon, while returning from class, I saw him standing at the very spot where he had once rescued me and made me promise not to take risks again. My heart skipped a beat. As if pulled by a magnetic force, I walked toward him.

"'Hello, how are you?' he asked with a gentle smile.

"Once again, my tongue betrayed me. My eyes were caught in his large, mesmerizing gaze, and I could not speak. After a moment, I noticed he was holding a packet of sweets. He offered me one and said warmly, 'I cleared two stages of my exams. I am confident about the third and final interview, for which I am leaving tomorrow.'

"Joy flooded me at his happiness. I finally managed to congratulate him and wished him success in the final stage.

"After a brief silence, he said quietly, 'I am leaving, and perhaps I will not return here for a long time.' The joy in my heart dimmed instantly at the thought of his departure.

"We stood there, looking at each other, each second precious and heavy with unspoken words. At last, he spoke. 'I will always pray for your safety and happiness. Promise me that you will never give up in life. If ever you feel lost and helpless, remember that somewhere on this earth there is someone who always wishes you well. Some meetings are short but precious, everlasting in their own way. That is all I can tell you.'

"'Thank you,' I whispered. My heart was full, my eyes brimming with tears. Mustering courage, I looked up and said, 'My heart will always pray for your success and happiness. And thank you for these precious memories.'

"He held my hand for a moment, looked deep into my eyes, and said softly, 'I am happy I met you. Let us part with these pure and blissful memories in our hearts.'

"And with that, he was gone."

She fell silent after sharing this chapter of her life, and I felt as though I had been walking with her down memory lane, visualizing every scene as it unfolded. After a short pause, I said gently, "So, that was the end of your love story?"

She shook her head. "No, it was the beginning."

"What exactly do you mean by that?" I asked, curious.

She smiled faintly. "Since I have shared a part of my life journey with someone for the first time, let me conclude it as well." I leaned closer, eager to hear more.

"My life went through many changes after his departure," she continued. "I joined the same institute as an instructor where I had once been a student, and I also started teaching young children from the neighbourhood. Slowly, the situation at home improved. My father's business picked up, and my mother never missed a chance to remind me how right she had been in choosing my path.

"The roof corner remained my favourite refuge. It gave me a sense of calm, as though someone was silently watching over me with deep understanding. Then, one day, my mother announced that she had found a suitable match for me. The groom was the only son of his parents, had a secure government job, and owned a house. According to her, I would be happy and well looked after post marriage.

"Once again, she decided the course of my life without asking for my consent. But by then, I was beyond protest. Nothing seemed to matter anymore. When my younger brother questioned her about why I was to marry someone almost nine years older, she brushed it aside, saying age made no difference. Perhaps, she added vaguely, he had not married earlier because he was destined to be my partner. I could sense something was being concealed.

"A few days before the wedding, I met one of my old school classmates. She revealed that my future husband had once been deeply in love with a girl of another caste and had insisted on marrying her. His mother, however, threatened to take her own life if he did so. Like many mothers, she had her ways. Broken by her threats, he vowed never to marry. But years later, the same mother used the same threat to force him into marriage—with me.

"In that moment, I understood the truth behind the age gap and realized that both of us were victims of circumstances shaped by our mothers' decisions. I had to give up my ambition of higher studies, and he had to give up the girl he loved.

"My marriage was a low-key affair, attended only by close relatives. A new chapter began in my life without any fanfare. My husband made it clear from the beginning that, as the only son, it was his duty to carry forward the family line as his parents wished. I never asked him about his past, and he never told me.

"Within a few months, I was pregnant with my first child. I don't know what made me so vulnerable at that time. Perhaps it was the weight of hormones, or perhaps the sense of insecurity. One day, tears overcame me, and I fell asleep crying. In my dream, I suddenly saw that familiar, loving face. He looked at me with such empathy, no words spoken, no touch exchanged, only that deep, consoling gaze. I woke up startled, wondering why this dream had come to me after so many years.

"'Never give up'—I remembered his last words. Could he somehow sense my loneliness, and through that dream reminded me that his thoughts were still with me? After that, I felt an unexplainable calm. Slowly, the woman in me began to change. The shy, timid girl gave way to someone stronger, more assertive.

"My in-laws wanted a grandson and prayed for it constantly, but I no longer let that burden weigh on me. The final days of my pregnancy were tough. I even refused to go to my parents' house, as was customary, because I felt strangely detached. I wanted to face it all in my own way.

"My sleep became restless, and strange dreams often disturbed me. In one such dream, I found myself standing at the edge of a deep gorge. On the other side stood a temple I longed to reach, but no matter how hard I tried, I could not cross. Suddenly, a hand reached out, grasped mine firmly, and pulled me across to safety. I knew instantly who it was. He gave me a brief, reassuring look before vanishing into the mist. After that dream, I felt certain everything would be alright.

"My first child was a daughter, and as I held her in my arms, I made a silent promise—I would never let her dreams die, as mine once had. Three years later, my second daughter was born. I then decided I would not have any more children. By then, my husband had softened after becoming a father, and he agreed, though he asked me to keep this decision between us.

"On my insistence, both my daughters studied in the best school in our locality. I became their friend, philosopher, and guide. Together with the love of their parents and grandparents, they grew up in a happy, nurturing family. The elder one went on to become a doctor, and the younger chose teaching as her profession. Today, she is a much-loved lecturer in her college. Both found life partners of their choice and live contented lives.

"As for me, I finally achieved the freedom I had once longed for. With a group of friends, I now travel to places of my choice once or twice a year. My husband has ensured that I am financially secure, and I have no complaints—neither against life nor anyone in it. Looking back, I realise that whenever I stood at a crossroads or felt unsure, that voice embedded deep in my memory always guided me. It gave me courage, faith, and the strength to trust myself."

Her story made me forget my own worries for a while. As my journey neared its end, I asked her, "Why did you feel like sharing your deepest feelings with me?"

She smiled gently. "I don't know. I just wanted to."

"And if you ever meet him again, how will you react?" I asked.

She laughed softly. "We wouldn't even recognize each other. Time has changed me, and I'm sure it has changed him too. Do you remember that song from the old Hindi movie—*sirf ehsaas hai ye, rooh se mehsoos karo, pyar ko pyar hi rehne do koi naam na do* (It is only a feeling, feel it with your soul, let love remain love, don't give it a name)?"

"Yes," I said. "A lovely song. True love is to be felt with the soul. The moment it becomes physical, it becomes finite. And anything finite must end. Let it remain infinite."

My station arrived, and as I prepared to get down, she asked, "Do you believe in Lord Shiva?"

"Oh yes," I replied. "He is the Ultimate."

"Well then, I will pray for your mother the moment I enter his temple. I am sure she will survive."

I thanked her and stepped down. My mother lived for three more years after that. And this journey, this unexpected sharing of souls remains unforgettable to this day.

THE INDOMITABLE SPIRIT

Life has strange ways. It can take a complete turn without any warning, leaving one in a daze. The same happened with her.

After living a full life and bringing up her children to the best of their capacities, she and her husband decided to spend their post-retirement years in a semi-urban village. After a few initial hiccups, they settled there comfortably. By then, all three children were well established in their own lives, so there was little to worry about.

With ample land around their home, she turned to her hobby of gardening. Soon, the garden bloomed with flowers of every variety and colour, lending the house a cheerful, lively charm. The villagers, along with relatives who had lived in that small town all their lives, gradually accepted the couple. Some of the women, who were curious about city life, began visiting her, asking questions about the ways of people in big cities. She liked their simplicity and naturalness. Three blissful years passed this way, with children visiting during vacations and filling the house with joy.

Then one fine morning, without any warning, the master of the house passed away peacefully. Life changed in an instant. She had faced many ups and downs before, victories and failures, but this was shattering. It came without any mental preparation, leaving her shaken to the core.

The children came rushing home, and the whole village gathered to share their grief and lend support. After a fortnight, when the rituals were over, her children collectively decided that she would stay with them, moving from one home to another as she preferred. No one asked her opinion. Too weary to resist, she complied with their wishes and left with her eldest son.

He instructed his family and staff to look after Ma well, to give her rest and comfort. Gradually, life settled again, and she tried to adjust to her new circumstances. But she could not ignore how different things felt now.

Earlier, whenever she and her husband visited their children, everything was planned in advance. The grandchildren had their vacations, and small trips were arranged. Everyone was relaxed, and time passed happily until it was time to return. Now, however, time loomed heavily. The household was busy with its own routine. She was greeted with customary questions. "How are you, Ma? Is everything okay?" followed by a few general comments about the weather or work. Some days even those brief exchanges were missing.

She tried to spend time with her two grandsons but soon realized they too were caught in a tightly packed schedule: school, homework, tuition, extracurriculars. Sometimes she pitied them, remembering the carefree childhood her own children once had. But life changes with time, and everyone must go with the flow.

To pass her days, she took to reading newspapers or whatever books she could find. Yet, after some time, small ailments began troubling her—stomach aches, headaches, insomnia. After much complaining, her son finally took her for a medical check-up. The doctor said it was nothing serious, just age-related issues.

She wondered, was she disappointed by that verdict? In the past, she had never given her health much thought. Home remedies had always been her solution for minor ailments, and she had taught her children to follow a healthy lifestyle, to avoid doctors unless absolutely necessary. But now, she felt trapped, caught in a web of her own thoughts, her body and mind no longer working with the same resilience.

Whenever she overheard her son and daughter-in-law talking about the rising cost of living, or how difficult it was to make ends meet, she began to think of herself as a burden in their eyes. One day, she suggested giving them a small monthly allowance. Her son laughed it off, saying in jest that if she really wanted to contribute, she could pay for the entire family's New Year trip. In earlier times, she would have laughed right back, replying, "No way, son, you both earn well. I will contribute but forget about paying for the whole trip." Now, however, she felt tongue tied. What if he really meant it?

In her earlier life she had never attached much importance to money. The family did not have wealth in abundance, but by spending wisely and cutting down on unnecessary demands, especially their own, she and her husband had managed well. Their children were taught to value needs over wants, and that upbringing eventually made them all independent and capable.

Why then was she, who had once been so secure, now plagued by this sense of insecurity?

A few months later, her daughter took her home for a while. The change felt welcome. The youngest child there had just started school and quickly grew attached to his grandmother. He loved her bedtime stories and insisted on sleeping beside her at night. For her, it was like reliving the old times, sweet and comforting. But good times are short lived. Soon her daughter complained that the boy was getting late for school because he refused to wake up early after sleeping with her. With no other choice, she agreed to step aside.

The children did spend some time with her, but their lives were busy with swimming classes, dance lessons, and schoolwork. When she tried to help with household chores, her daughter gently stopped her, urging her to rest and not bother about anything. Gradually she began to feel like an unwanted guest, someone being tolerated rather than needed. Even her suggestions on raising children or simple remedies for common ailments were politely dismissed as outdated.

Her youngest son, the most ambitious of the three, was abroad on a company project. He often shared his desire to settle there permanently and looked for opportunities to do so. Whenever he called, he would say, "Ma, once I settle down, I will call you here. There is nothing left in our country, you will enjoy a lot here." She had once loved travelling, but only within her own country. That small dream had never been fulfilled. When her children were young, they had promised to take her on trips to see new places, but now they were caught up in their own lives and problems. After two months she returned to her son's house, and life moved on.

She felt as though she were trapped in a large cage where measured amounts of light, air, food, and water were provided only to keep her going. Everyone remained oblivious to the loneliness gnawing at her heart. Someone once said that old age and childhood share many similarities, and it is true. In both phases, there is a constant craving for something more.

One day, tired of the bland food, she asked the maid to bring her a spicy snack and slipped some money into her hand. The poor maid got caught, and all hell broke loose. Her son and daughter-in-law were furious with the girl and fired her on the spot. In tears, the maid begged forgiveness. That was the breaking point. She confronted her son directly. "Why are you punishing her when the fault is mine?"

"Ma, your fault was that you acted without the knowledge of the guardians of the house," her son replied.

"And son, who am I then? I thought I was the eldest in the family, a guardian myself. When did I become an outsider?" she asked, her voice firm and hurt.

For a moment, silence filled the house. Then her words softened the anger. The maid was forgiven and allowed to stay. After a long time, she felt like herself again. She realized she could still decide for herself. How had she forgotten that? She had always been a loving and giving person, but lately something had made her bitter and restless. Perhaps she was to be blamed for letting that happen, but no more of it now.

The next day, when a close relative called to ask how she was, she told him to come and meet her in person. She also asked him to bring two return tickets, as she had decided to go back.

"But *bhabhi*, how will you manage? At this age you should be doing *aaram*," he said.

She laughed lightly and chided him. "Will they not look after me there? I have had enough rest. My body parts are getting rusted. But if you cannot come, it is fine, I will manage alone."

Alarmed, he promised to come at once.

Her unexpected guest surprised everyone at the house. When she told her son she wanted to return to the village for some time, he protested, reminding her of the hardships of life there. Calmly, she replied that it was only a short break, and he need not worry, as she would be back soon.

What she did not reveal was that she had resolved to start a new chapter of her life. Once back in the village, she quietly chalked out her plan. It was tough at first, but slowly everything fell into place. Her beloved garden began to bloom again, bursting with flowers of every shade and fragrance. Neighbours often came to borrow flowers for puja, and she was happy to share.

Her days found a rhythm. She began with a morning walk, a little yoga, and then her gardening. To her surprise, her minor health troubles vanished. Yet she still felt there was something missing.

One fine morning, a wealthy villager asked to buy all her flowers for a special occasion. At first, she refused payment, but when he insisted, she accepted. She did not need the money, but after some thought, she bought picture books and coloured pencils with it. She had noticed how poor children often looked longingly at their peers who went to school, and an idea took root in her mind.

Thus began her little school with five eager children. They were mesmerized by the colorful books, and she felt a deep sense of fulfilment watching wonder light up their innocent eyes.

The numbers grew quickly, as the children began receiving free notebooks, pencils, and storybooks. She started with pictures, then letters, and soon they were learning joyfully, eager to please the teacher who adored them. Teaching had always come naturally to her. Even with her own children, she had loved helping them with their schoolwork and introducing them to books and activities of their choice.

She opened a small account dedicated to this endeavour, drawing from the income she made selling flowers and adding a bit from her personal savings. Parents of the children also contributed whatever little they could. Over time, the number of her students grew so much that some parents preferred sending their children to her rather than the village school. What began as a small initiative became a full-time passion.

Her life brimmed with purpose once more. Surrounded by children, she felt as though she were back with her grandchildren, only this time in far greater numbers. Relatives and neighbours began seeking her advice, not only about children but about family matters too. Without realizing it, she had become indispensable to many.

The elderly of the village requested her to engage older children as well, and she gladly agreed. She also shared her method of producing organic manure for her flowers, demonstrating it simply so that others could adopt it easily. Soon, many followed her example.

Her days were spent mingling with both young and adolescent minds, and this kept her refreshed. The children and teenagers confided in her freely, and without noticing, she had become a counsellor. Listening to their concerns, guiding them with patience, and watching them bloom brought her immense satisfaction. Now she had no complaints with life, nor with anyone.

I met her during one of my project assignments, which focused on the changing scenario in Indian villages. When an acquaintance asked me if I would like to meet a seventy-year-young woman who was doing remarkable work for her community, I eagerly agreed. Meeting her was an experience in itself. She radiated vitality, charm, and confidence.

I could not help myself. "What is the secret of your energy?" I asked.

And then, as though opening a long-locked chest, she began to narrate her life's journey.

At the end, I finally asked the question that lingered in my mind. "Are you still hurt by the behaviour of your children?"

"No," she said softly. "In fact, they were not at fault, nor was I. It was the circumstances that led to everything that happened. One thing life has taught me is that every person behaves or reacts according to the circumstances they are facing. Change the circumstances, and you will see the behaviour of the same person change as well. It is rightly said we are all puppets in the hands of our circumstances.

"The saints develop the power to rise above the influence of circumstances, which is why they remain unaffected. But a common person flounders. In fact, I love my children even more now, because through all of this I discovered a part of myself I had never known. And God gave me the opportunity to work on it.

"I feel wiser now, free of my insecurities, and unafraid of death. Come what may, I am ready to face it. When I depart from this world, it will be without any burden on my conscience. My final journey will be light and fearless."

I sat there, deeply moved, listening to the calm conviction in her voice. Her indomitable spirit filled the room, and as I rose to leave, I bid her farewell with a sense of reverence in my heart.

THE WOMAN

"Why don't you visit a place nearby? There is a saint there. Although a family man, he is full of wisdom, and people say he once stayed with a guru near the Himalayas for a long time," quipped my friend.

I was feeling low after the death of Ma, perhaps a little guilty as well. When aged parents pass away, regrets always linger. You find yourself asking if you failed to give them the time they needed most, which is often more valuable than medical facilities or material comforts. For a change of environment, I decided to go.

It was a small ashram with a few rooms where one could stay by donating whatever they wished. The serenity of the place calmed me instantly, and I slept soundly for the first time in many days.

I have always loved observing people, and in the next two days I quietly watched the rhythm of life there. Mornings began with discussions, followed by two hours meant for breakfast, bathing, and other chores. Afternoons were quieter, with fewer visitors. Lunch was served, after which people rested, often taking short naps. Evenings were the most crowded, when many locals came in, followed by a simple dinner.

Everything was remarkably well managed, which intrigued me. I never once saw the master, Guruji, giving instructions to the staff or his followers. Visitors came with varied intentions. Some sought solutions to personal problems. Some engaged in discussions on social and political issues. A few, only a select few, came with a genuine quest for spirituality and stayed back for late-night sessions with the master.

With some quiet enquiry, I discovered that the smooth running of the ashram was overseen by the lady of the house, whose presence was subtle, almost invisible. She was everywhere and nowhere at the same time, appearing only when needed, never drawing attention to herself. Most often, I saw her in the kitchen, offering a helping hand to anyone who required it.

It was in that kitchen that I first grew acquainted with her, joining in to help with small chores. At first, she gently asked me to leave things to the staff, but gradually, as we grew more comfortable with each other, she allowed me to assist. If ever I was late, I noticed a quiet relief in her eyes when she spotted me.

One day, as we worked side by side, I asked her about her life. She told me she had been married young, as was customary in those days. Children were born one after another, and life moved on with its share of highs and lows, until suddenly, one day, her husband disappeared.

She was left with five small children to feed and no one to rely on but herself. "I was suddenly at a crossroad. I did not know what to do. People began talking. Some asked if there had been discord or a fight that led to the man of the house abandoning us.

I had no words. Brought up in a traditional way, questioning the master of the house never arose. How could I think of fighting back or making demands of my own? Things were very tough," she confided quietly.

"All I knew was that my husband had a spiritual inclination. He often attended such gatherings, and I never objected. But if he wanted to leave, the least he could have done was to tell me. There were so many unanswered questions," she said, pausing, lost in thought.

She grew silent for a while, her gaze fixed somewhere in the past. I asked gently how she had faced such abandonment and raised her children alone.

"You know," she said at last with a faint, distant smile, "life gives you surprises to test your tenacity. I had no idea I possessed that strength, but I discovered it when I needed it most."

All I had at that time was a house, some land being cultivated by others who were honest enough to give us our share, and a small amount of savings. There was no time to sit and cry. My children were my first priority, so I focused on raising them. To continue their education, many things were cut down to the bare minimum. Our food became extremely simple. Apart from their school uniforms, I taught them to manage with only a pair of clothes. Luckily, they understood without complaining."

She paused, then added, "Life was hard, but it taught us the meaning of integrity and honesty, and how these two virtues help you survive adversity. I rented out the extra rooms, and I began preparing tiffin for poor children, charging them according to their means. It gave me a purpose and brought me inner peace."

I asked her, "When and how did the master return?"

"How, I cannot tell you," She said quietly, "but it was after six years. By then, my eldest was in college and the others were a few years behind. One fine morning he was back. My eldest son saw him first. Surprised, he came inside and informed us."

"What did you and the children feel at that sudden moment?" I asked.

"I had mixed feelings. It was neither happiness nor sorrow, but a sense of relief for the sake of the children. As for them, the younger two did not recognize him at all, while the other three were hesitant in the beginning. But gradually, everything settled, and life returned to normal."

"You never asked him why he had done this?"

She sighed. "When the eldest confronted him, he simply said he had found his guru and had been with him all those years. Now he had returned on his guru's command. He had not informed anyone before leaving because he felt nobody would have allowed him to go. That was all."

I was surprised. "Was that not a callous act? Would a woman be accepted in such a situation? Never. Our society has very different standards. You never felt like confronting him yourself?"

"No," she said firmly. "What was the use? Sometimes an event that feels life-shattering in one moment becomes superfluous with the passage of time."

Both of us sat in silence for a while. Then, breaking it, she said softly, "Looking back, I feel everything happens for a purpose. We are often unable to see the larger canvas with our limited vision. I was a timid, shy housewife who hardly ever stepped outside alone. But through that experience, I learned to reinvent myself. I discovered a resilience and tenacity I never knew I possessed."

Her eyes softened as she continued, "Now my children have their own lives. They are proud of their father, because of the love and respect he receives in society."

I asked quietly, "And what about you? Are they not proud of you?" For a moment, I thought I saw a wistful look in her eyes.

She smiled gently. "I never asked them. Once the children learn to use their wings, the mother bird is happy and does not think of calling them back. I have practiced the art of zero expectations, so I am content."

I looked around her room. In one corner was a puja space with The Ramayana, The Bhagavad Geeta, and a few other religious texts arranged neatly. Nearby stood a small bookshelf filled with literary masterpieces. Noticing my gaze, she said, "I love books. They are my best companions."

I asked, "Tell me one thing. Although you manage everything here in the ashram, people hardly give you the respect and reverence you deserve. Does that not hurt?"

“Nothing hurts me now,” she said with serene calm. “I am at peace with myself, and the Almighty is always with me. What more do I need?”

I then asked why she rarely sat in the durbar of Guruji. With a smile she replied, “Most of the time, those gatherings are filled with arguments. Everyone tries to outwit the other. Why should I waste my time? I prefer to listen when a true spiritual discourse takes place.”

Her words left me lighter, more at peace.

After two days, I decided to return home. When I went to bid farewell, she seemed a little disappointed. “Why so soon? I thought you liked this place,” she said.

“I loved staying here,” I replied, “but I too have some unfinished duties waiting for me.”

“I learned a lot from you, so thank you.” On an impulse, I touched her feet. She was touched, and with moist eyes she asked me to come back whenever I wished.

On my return journey, I halted briefly at my acquaintance’s place, the one who had advised me to visit the ashram. “How was it?” he asked. “You look so serene. It seems the man is truly spiritual.”

“The woman,” I replied with a quiet smile.